Conversations

Conversations

Marilyn Holman

Copyright © 2023 Marilyn Holman

The moral right of the author has been asserted.

Apart from any fair dealing for the purposes of research or private study, or criticism or review, as permitted under the Copyright, Designs and Patents Act 1988, this publication may only be reproduced, stored or transmitted, in any form or by any means, with the prior permission in writing of the publishers, or in the case of reprographic reproduction in accordance with the terms of licences issued by the Copyright Licensing Agency. Enquiries concerning reproduction outside those terms should be sent to the publishers.

This is a work of fiction. Names, characters, businesses, places, events and incidents are either the products of the author's imagination or used in a fictitious manner. Any resemblance to actual persons, living or dead, or actual events is purely coincidental.

Matador
Unit E2 Airfield Business Park,
Harrison Road, Market Harborough,
Leicestershire. LE16 7UL
Tel: 0116 2792299
Email: books@troubador.co.uk
Web: www.troubador.co.uk/matador
Twitter: @matadorbooks

ISBN 978 1803136 677

British Library Cataloguing in Publication Data.
A catalogue record for this book is available from the British Library.

Printed and bound in Great Britain by 4edge Limited
Typeset in 10.5pt Aldine401 BT by Troubador Publishing Ltd, Leicester, UK

Matador is an imprint of Troubador Publishing Ltd

*Dedicated to Debbie, David, Cathy, Pauline
and all who follow them, "My Family"*

Conversations

Miscellaneous	**1**
China Tea	3
Don's Garden	5
Home	7
Flight	9
Flowers	10
Insight	12
I Am Ill	14
Memory Lane	17
High and Dry	19
My Pal	22
Death of a Guardroom Cat	24
Religion	27
True Love	28
The Dream	29
What Is Pain?	30
The Human Abattoir	32
Anecdotes	**39**
My Brother-in-Law	41
Christmas Present	43
Dentures	45
Bicycle	47
Camping	51

Letters	**71**
Hi Cousins, Thank You So Much…	73
Hi Everybody, I Am Still on Shank's Pony…	77
Hi Cousins, So Pleased to Hear You Are Enjoying Life…	81
Hi Cousins, My First Date for Operation…	84
The New Secretary	89
The Editor 1	91
Topical	**93**
Immigration: The Migrant's Story	95
The Native's Story	101
The Solution	106
Pandemic	108
Gender	113

MISCELLANEOUS

Miscellaneous

China Tea

Do you remember when you invited me to lunch at the Georgian *Tearooms*? They were prestigious tearooms providing many specialty teas and were frequented by the genteel fraternity from the local and surrounding areas, and knowing my penchant for China tea you escorted me through the impressive wrought-iron gates and up to the wisteria-covered entrance.

I thought to myself, I must impress this self-assured courteous man of the world, and entered with a flourish! We sat at the table towards the centre of the room and the waitress appeared to take our order.

As you did not drink tea yourself you ordered coffee with your cream and jam scone, then it was my turn: "Could I have a pot of Rose Pouchong tea, please?"

"I'm sorry, we do not have Rose Pouchong."

"Never mind, I'll have Oolong instead."

"We don't have Oolong either," was the reply; by this time you were shuffling uncomfortably in your chair!

"Well, what China teas do you have?"

"Lapsang Souchong."

"No, thank you, too smoky for me, just bring me any green China tea that you have, please."

She shuffled off, and the hum of conversation and clink of teacups was very soothing around us.

Eventually the silver tea tray arrived complete with cream jug, hot water, very elegant teapot and tea strainer.

"Best let it brew a minute," I said. "Don't you wait, you carry on with your coffee."

After a minute or two I lifted the lid on the teapot and, taking the teaspoon from the cup and saucer, gave the tea a good stir; unfortunately, when I removed the spoon I found that in fact the contents were teabags on strings which had wound themselves all around the handle of the spoon rather like a bird's nest!

The look of embarrassment on your face said it all, and one by one the clinking of cups around us ceased, as did the conversations, and all eyes fixed on me, awaiting my next move!

"Well," I said, "I think that's enough stirring," and with a flourish I threw the teabag-entwined spoon back in the teapot and closed the lid, firmly hoping that it would not block the spout when I poured out the tea! And so the meal progressed in uncomfortable silence and I was whisked away at the earliest opportunity followed by much tut-tutting and whispering from amongst the clinking teacups, never to be invited back there again!

Miscellaneous

Don's Garden

I hope you like the garden, it's the best that I can do to make it a memorial that's good enough for you…

You are always right here with me when I am tending to the flowers or sweeping up the windblown leaves in between the autumn showers.

I imagine that I can see you on the garden seat out there beneath the rose and trellis hedge contemplating all that's fair.

The sparrows' dust bath in the border, there must be thirty now or more, nesting in the honeysuckle hedge over the greenhouse door.

Remember how they twitter whilst they are waiting to be fed at five o'clock in the morning as I tumble out of bed.

They come down to the window for sultanas on the sill and peep inside to see if you are watching over them still.

The dragonflies have hatched this year after three years in the deep; our little pond has many hidden secrets that she keeps to surprise us every spring and summer day to come, if we have the time to contemplate where Nature makes her home.

The summer flowers are all in bloom, it's looking pretty now, you'll have to see it through my eyes as I know you will somehow.

The grass is looking green and lush, the palm tree straighter than before, the lavenders and heathers full of honeybees once more.

There's butterflies aplenty on the buddleia out the back, and insects, weird and wonderful, along the gravel track!

I miss you here beside me to enjoy our little space, but I feel you're never far away from this, our 'special place'.

For this must be part of heaven, the nearest we can get to the creation of our 'Eden' whilst earthbound here and yet…

There is something missing from this place as I sit and watch this view.

Sadly it does not have my heart because that is still with you…

Miscellaneous

Home

What does home mean to me?

Home is a little bungalow that smiles at me through her lace curtains as I approach her.

It is where the gate scrapes the ground a little as I enter this domain of mine.

The garden path is full of summer flowers now fading and the autumn leaves are just beginning to fall, so Mother Nature herself is relaxing on a bountiful diet of colour, texture, form and scent before she slips into her winter slumber.

As I turn the key in the front door an air of peace and tranquillity engulfs me and says, "Come on in and welcome."

It is silent now since that fateful day my husband died here in my arms, but this little sanctuary seems to envelope both me and his presence…

Every smile, tear and kiss is imprinted in every room, and as I wander around I stop to consider what this little 'home' represents to me…

Not just shelter from the elements: a roof, a kitchen, a sitting room, two bedrooms and a bathroom.

It is a builder of dreams and hopes, of shared sunlit days and starry nights, a safe haven for a troubled soul, and a place of laughter and joy when family and friends come to visit.

This little home doesn't ask for much, just a lick of paint now and again and windows kept bright and shiny to let the sunlight in, and to close the curtains on a cold wet night and snuggle up safe and warm.

Her floral boundaries provide habitats for birds, hedgehogs, and a host of insects and butterflies that come to share this home with us.

How lucky I am to live here, and in the eventual ending of my time here I am sure that this little bungalow will smile on the next residents to come here, and maybe they will feel our happiness here in the very fabric that makes this 'HOME'.

Miscellaneous

Flight

The sky is very blue today; the clouds are wisps of white.
The contrails criss-cross back and forth from great
 metallic birds in flight.
Their destinations are unknown to earthbound watchers
 here.
But time and deadlines, all a rush, take precedence, I fear.
And then a buzzard comes into view beneath that
 canopy.
He circles around above the trees so effortlessly.
He doesn't need a plane to catch to take him on his way.
Just spreads his wings upon a thermal and slowly sails
 away.

Miscellaneous

Flowers

Why do we call them 'wild' flowers or 'cultivated' ones?

Flowers are like people: some shy with small flowers, some big, bold and brassy.
Some sleek and sensuous with intoxicating perfume, some elegant and graceful and refined.
Some bullies with thorns or poisons to wound and hurt.

Many others need support by clinging on to the nearest available strong ally to reach their eventual potential.
There are many squabbles for available space, and include suffocating or strangling the neighbours!

There are many nationalities i.e. bulbs, corms, tubers, seeds, cuttings and rhizomes.
Some will germinate easily and wide, whilst others need much attention to reproduce with special requirements to help them.

Some prefer bright sunlight to show off their colours,
whilst others prefer to stay in the shade and quietly
bloom on their own where there is less attention
to bother them, and some even grow in the winter
months when there is less competition about.

But a strange thing happens when all these flowers are
put into the same place and tended and cared for in
their own little patch: they all mix together to form a
cacophony of colour, perfume, shape and size, each
flowering in its own season and time to form what
we call a 'garden'.

What a triumph it would be if people could live like the
flowers united in time and space.
What a 'garden' that would be!

Miscellaneous

Insight

Just because my eyes are blind do not think I cannot see.
I have a greater gift of sight within my memory.
To me you are forever young and thus will always be
in my imagination, because the world stands still for me.
I see no age or getting old but pictures clear and bright,
of times gone by of youth and strength within my 'special sight'.
I do not need your pity or sense your sorrowful glance.
I am still the man I always was if given half a chance!
I have a new perspective now on my existence without sight,
I have the glow of brightness from my innermost source of light
This insight serves me very well when daily obstacles persist.
The fact that I cannot see them means that they just do not exist!
Whatever Nature takes from us she gives back another way.

My vision of life is different now but I have known a
   brighter day.
So which do you think that I would choose if I ever had
   to decide,
to be able to look around me again or to have you here
   by my side?

Miscellaneous

I Am Ill

What am I doing here today? Well, really I'm not sure.
I thought this was the place you come to when
 searching for a cure.

The ambulance crew were helpful: "Can you walk out
 on your own? We can't get the vehicle right up here
 past all those roadwork cones."

Eventually a trolley came trundling up the path.
Luckily I had not emerged from a nice relaxing bath.

The cold air hit me with an easterly blast that took my
 breath away,
as I was wheeled across the cobbled stones in the early
 light of day!

I had visited the doctor as I was not well the previous day.
I had a full ten minutes for my symptoms to relay.

The conversation went like this: "Now what's wrong with you today?"
"Well, if I knew that I'd diagnose myself, old chum," I say.

So here I am, midst flashing lights and sirens on my way to that blessed place called 'Hospital' to the emergency bay.

Awaiting me in uniforms of different colours bright,
an array of eager hospital staff working hard to get it right!

Luckily by daybreak I actually had a bed on a ward.
Now this was better and more comfortable, I felt more reassured.

I laid there quiet in my bed, hoping to get some sleep.
I closed my eyes and drifted off, then *BEEP BEEP BEEP BEEP BEEP!*

Another trolley appeared on the ward, this one had a lid.
A fellow inmate in the opposite bed called out,
   "Cheerio, old Syd."

I tried again to settle down and kept breathing as well as I might.
"Don't worry, old chap," the doctor said, "we'll be with you tomorrow night."

The pills arrived, but I just didn't care, I swallowed them all without moan.
It wasn't till later I realised that my deaf aid battery had gone!

Peace, perfect peace then prevailed, the silence was sublime.
Quietly serenaded by the gurgling sounds emanating from this stomach of mine.

I wonder what tomorrow will bring in this anxious state of mind.
At least I can't see what's on my plate – there are advantages to being blind!

I think I'll stick to jacket spud, they can't do much to that!
A bit of carbohydrate will stop me feeling flat.

I could go on with this lament, but latest news to tell:
Doc's had a breakdown in the lane so we're all off as well.

Miscellaneous

Memory Lane

I plan a trip down Memory Lane, a place I seldom go;
the crossing can be dangerous with hidden depths below.

The pathway twists and turns a lot and sometimes I get lost,
but with my guide beside me I will find a way to cross.

At indecision I turn left and take the wider trail;
this one leads on to Hope and Strength if I can navigate through Fail.

There is a little shady place called Rest-a-While Near Here,
but if I stay there for too long I'll lose my way, I fear.

So I will keep on travelling on this precarious way
until I come to that big climb called Hang-on-Ridge someday.

If I can reach towards the top, to that special place I know,
I may catch a glimpse of Peace of Mind stretching out below.

It's green and lush with forests, but watch out
for all the thorns of doubt and insecurity where tragedy was born…

But somewhere through this tangled route if I keep going through this part,
I know the best is yet to come, I can feel it in my heart.

When I make my destination, as one day I surely may, before me Love is waiting,
I will reach that view someday…

Whatever trials and tribulations may have followed me all through,
my Epic Memories journey was to finish here with you…

Miscellaneous

High and Dry

Samuel Pepys, Secretary to the Admiralty a few hundred years ago, said, "When a shippe hath been at sea awhile, her bones are weary, likewise her men, thus 'tis provident to return to harbour and resteth awhile" (or words to that effect). The Admiralty certainly agrees; however, they insist that the men come back – 'On Time'!

Thus it came to pass, my battered Corvette, tired of it all, came to rest her bones at Sheerness. I and four others (for some reason never fathomed) were in 'temp' accommodation (Wildfire Barracks). With true RN zeal and aptitude we 'carried on'. Being countrymen at heart and true British sportsmen, we acquired a brace of polecat ferrets (well hidden near the butcher's shop). We 'found' sail twine and brass sail eyelets and knitted rabbit nets. Two shotguns completed our sporting tackle. Thus we would at opportune times set off to shoot wildfowl or ferret the rabbits in local pastures, etc. We were, after all, being 'patriotic' in supplementing naval rations with wild-caught, natural food; we were, in fact, assisting the 'war effort' by cutting down on the nation's food! This was not even mentioned on our record sheets, nor even appreciated!

One night ashore I met a bright young ATS. CPL, she was on a nearby A/A site, Island of Grain, and I proposed to her (after a few rums) and was rejected. She said that I had a face that only my mother could love; however, she did volunteer the information that her section was having a dance on the site and we would be welcome to attend.

We 'arranged' to use a 'trotboat' (Admiralty property). Four of us in greatcoats pushed off in a good spring flood tide. We made fast to the bollards on the jetty, found the gun-site and were soon dancing away like puppets on a string. At 22.30hrs purple alarm sounded (V1 rockets): flying bombs passing over. We were ordered off the site. Rain poured down, and, soaking wet, we took refuge in a telephone box some distance away. Sleep was impossible with three other persons standing up, especially as the 'phone' dial was pressed firmly into my neck. Cramp set in, our uniforms had 'set' into a box-like shape, and gunfire from ship and shore created shrapnel all around us, so we fled from our telephone box down the nearest country lane until we reached an empty air-raid shelter and fell asleep on the stone deck.

Dawn broke.

"My Christ," I shouted, "we're covered in feathers."

Someone had been plucking duck, turkey and geese – we were plastered! Still covered with 'fluff' we made our way to the jetty only to find the trotboat was high and dry, hanging from the bollards, and the tide well out!

Royal Marine constables took us into custody. "Had to, mateys, the dockyard super is looking for his boat."

We were weighed off and charged with 'Out of bounds in a Garrison area', 'Improperly dressed', 'Conduct Prejudicial', and, most serious of all, 'Hazarding a Naval Vessel'!

My defending officer said, "You might as well have run the Ark Royal aground, it's the same charge and punishment."

Captain (Wildfire), of old school, said to me, "It's evident to me that you were the ringleader as coxswain of the vessel. Your record is only equalled by that of Dick Turpin. You think the Royal Navy has been formed for your sole use – well, it hasn't! If I could impose flogging or keelhauling I would do so; unfortunately, these punishments are no longer allowed. Disrated to the rank of AB, to be drafted to a more active theatre of war, and get rid of those bloody ferrets!"

Miscellaneous

My Pal

My little pal with crooked paw, I don't even know your name
You just appear when I come here every visit the same
I sit upon my old log seat beneath our little tree
Beside the grave of that brave man who was the best of me
You seem to sense my sadness as you curl up by my side
I'm sure you try to tell me that you know that he has died
You put that old head on my knee and sit there quiet and calm
As if to say, don't worry cos I'm only down at the farm
And I will pass here every day to keep him company
Until the day you join him here, then you will both be free…
And maybe someday someone new will pass along this way

And they might see an old black dog with a crooked paw that day
Curled up by the old log seat beneath that little tree
Where you would come and rest that head gently upon my knee…
My Guardian of this special place where 'He' once softly trod
Little Keeper of my dear soul till we unite in God.

Miscellaneous

Death of a Guardroom Cat

It is with profound regret that I announce the death of Betty our guardroom cat.

Betty was our permanent 'night' roving picket; she performed her manifold duties without fear or favour, pay or any other service entitlement.

She was not a beautiful cat in the sense of animal conformation, nor was she a strictly honest cat! But she was a sober cat, good mother (no doubt descended from a long, distinguished line of RAAF mousers); indeed, her own squadrons of multi-coloured kittens are now scattered throughout service commands in Australia giving joy to countless children and comfort to lonely persons.

Her age I know not, but of her skill at 'mousing' or capturing a juicy guardroom steak I will readily testify. Betty saw numerous changes at the base, many postings and a rich variety of night guards. Her knowledge of guard commanders' temperaments was second to none, knowing whom to avoid or not; I swear she studied the unit guard rosters, for when well-known 'fiery' guard commanders came up on the list, she would be absent from her 'place of duty'. Now she is gone forever...

That great English scholar Dr Samuel Johnson would I know forgive me if I quoted his words on the loss of a friend (in this case Betty the cat): "Let us reflect that to lose an old friend is to be cut off from a great part of the little pleasure that our life allows, yet it is inevitable that all union with the inhabitants of Earth must in time be broken, and all the hopes that terminate here must end in disappointment such is the impermanence of relationships," and I would add, such is the life of a guardroom cat!

Alas, the sands of time had been running out for Betty; adverse reports concerning her had been entered by night guard commanders in the log book. These ranged from petty larceny of guard rations to propagation of fleas; at least thirteen witnesses could be called upon to swear an oath that these diabolical crimes were committed by Betty.

She could not answer her accusers, thus no defence was called upon to rebut these grave contraventions of Air Force and Health acts. Telephone calls were made to possible interested parties, but alas, reason dictated to sentiment 'Guilty' was the judgement and death by chloroform administration was the method of execution.

I tried hard to find another place and owner for Betty away from the base, but she looked at me as if to say, "You know cats better than that, old friend, any home, even your own, would not suffice, for the guardroom and its precincts is my real home. Perhaps the time is overdue for my journey into that land from whence no weary cats return. Do as you please, but just one thing, will it be painful?"

I assured her that it would be a gentle, soft sleep; she implied that her life had been a good one with no regrets. Often she had seen the morning sun bathing our base in liquid gold, and often at night she had seen the planets wheeling in the heavens above and heard the whisper of the wind amidst our tender unit grass. Many a dawn she had marked the distant flight of birds overhead, and likewise she could tell me many tales of unit 'goings-on' during her nightly patrols!

She asked, "Is it true, old friend, that the hand that created me will also compound into tiny atoms that hand which will soon destroy me?"

I could find no answer, thus she died…

Miscellaneous

Religion

Someone asked me, "What is your religion?" I answered them thus…

Nature is my place of worship, the trees are my cathedrals and the flowers are my blessings,

The birds are my songs of praise and the weeds are my sins,

The breeze is my breath of life and the sun is the light of my world,

The moon is the lantern in my darkness, the grassy bank my pillow and the whisper of the leaves my prayers,

The running stream is my communion wine and the fruits of the valley my bread of heaven,

And finally, the stars will be my pathway to Paradise…

Miscellaneous

True Love

You cannot make someone love you if they don't… any more than you can capture a butterfly and keep it trapped within your fingers, allowing it to see the flowers but unable to fly to them; rather, you marvel as it flies from flower to flower, and if you are lucky enough it may come to rest on your knee and stay awhile, giving you a memory that lasts forever…

So if I cannot make you happy, go and find someone who can because you deserve to be happy, and there are no bars on these windows or bolts on these doors to keep you here, because if I want you to be happy and 'really love you' I must let you go…

So take your freedom if you must and leave me the priceless memories of our precious love together untainted by jealousy, anger and hate, for how lucky I am to have known such a love; you are the dearest and the best of me, and if you would remember me, be it not with bitterness and hurt, but with warmth, laughter and 'True Love'.

Miscellaneous

The Dream

You came to me last night.

As you slipped into bed beside me your arms held me close and I felt your naked warmth against my body and the familiar scent of your aftershave permeated my pillow and once more we were the lovers that we always were to one another and a feeling of complete peace and love engulfed me as I drifted off into a deep, relaxed, sound sleep.

In the morning when I awoke, I turned towards you and you were gone!

Were you ever really here at all? But I can still smell the faint scent of you on my pillow, or is that just my imagination?

How can you be dead when you hold me so tightly and tenderly in your arms or did I join you for a while in your spirit world and our souls entwined before I came back to my world?

All I do know is that we two can never be parted whatever form our love takes, or was it just a dream after all…

Miscellaneous

What is Pain?

"How's your pain level?" I am asked that question after my latest surgical foray. "On a scale of one to ten, what would you say?"

Well, I think to myself, on a scale of one to ten I would say that 80% plus burns to the human body would undoubtedly be a ten. The amputation of a limb or any other major surgical life-changing operation most definitely a nine plus.

Now when it comes to my own 'operations' I would say maybe a six or seven on the scale, leaving the multitude of other conditions to vary between a one to six because everyone is different as to the degree of pain that they can bear.

Physical pain comes and goes in varying degrees and can be helped by various pain-relieving medications.

But, what about the mental, emotional or psychological pain, like the loss of someone very dear to you?

That pain NEVER goes away! The physical feeling of a heart tearing itself to pieces, or the feeling in the pit of the stomach when the realisation hits that no more will that person appear in the doorway, or sit in that armchair, or caress away your fears and anxieties of the day, who will laugh with you and together you become complete in yourself and each other.

When that is cruelly taken away you become 'lost' and, however hard you try to focus on a return to 'normality', it is constant remembrance in a thousand different ways: a song on the radio, finding a box of matches from a holiday hotel or a little note written or received on a special day.

You yearn so much for that presence that you believe that they are actually here with you and you talk to them in the belief that they can hear you and will contact you in some spiritual form.

When people say, "Oh, time is a great healer, you know" – sadly not in my case!

I can go about my daily routine and people will never know the depths of my pain because it is 'My Pain' to last the rest of my life and the only cure will be to join him!

What scale of pain is that, I wonder?

Miscellaneous

The Human Abattoir

This is a true account of one man's struggle against a regime of calculated involuntary euthanasia by a combination of people and strategies to bring to a conclusion a life that is considered expendable 'in their opinion'. As far as their accountability is concerned their guilt is hidden behind the curtain of national and local guidelines, and the culprits well shielded from any responsibility for their actions.

Don was not a young man and had been ill for some time with COPD (Chronic Obstructive Pulmonary Disease) and was reaching the final stages of this illness which both he and his wife were well aware of.

In 2014 he suffered a bout of pneumonia, and his GP at the time and a hospital consultant for geriatrics visited him at home and told him and his wife that he was dying and that he would be better off in hospital. Don shook his head and said no, and his wife agreed that he would stay at home, where she had nursed him throughout his illness and he wished to be there with her.

The GP and consultant then proceeded to fill in a TEP

(non-resuscitation form) on his behalf, which was left on the premises with him for 'reference purposes' along with a pack of drugs in a JIC, 'just in case', bag. On his way out the consultant was heard to say, "He won't last the night," to which the community matron present said, "You can't say that about Don, he is a fighter," and she came back to Don saying, "I am on holiday for ten days, but I will see you when I get back."

"Yes, you will," was his reply, and indeed, he did see her again on her return when she visited him: he was sitting in his chair with a big smile on his face, having recovered from pneumonia.

We now move on to 2016 and Don had had two years of reasonable quality of life including the odd trip out on his motorised scooter to watch the local cricket and bowls matches along the seafront, but was gradually reaching a stage where he was sleeping more and fading but was peaceful and calm at home with his wife, who administered his daily dose of twenty-three medications and kept him as comfortable as possible, making sure he had a good diet and no pressure sores, clean and neat and interested in life going on around him in a bright and happy atmosphere.

Eventually, his pain increased and his wife contacted the GP surgery and the local Hospice Charity team, who had been visiting him on a regular basis. His wife told the GP that his pain relief needed increasing so could she increase his maintenance morphine dosage and/or his breakthrough morphine, neither of which had reached their maximum dosage at that stage.

The GP and the local Hospice Charity specialist nurse called to see Don, and then a decision was made between them all as to the next move; his wife was not consulted at this time as to what they were going to do to her husband and he refused to go into the local hospice, and his wife agreed that he would stay at home to die in the surroundings that he knew and loved.

The 19th August was momentous because the local Hospice Charity nurse specialist and a community nurse appeared as Don's wife was preparing his morning medications and she was told that he would not be requiring any of his medications anymore, and when she protested that they included twenty-four-hour oxygen, nebulisers, cortico-steroids and other medications that would cause withdrawal symptoms if stopped abruptly, she was told that what they were going to give him would 'compensate' for all that and he would not require nourishment or fluids.

So from that moment on all of Don's means of survival were taken away from him and he was put on a syringe driver and 30mg of diamorphine administered twice a day. This was three times the potency of the previous morphine he had been taking and threw him into hallucinations and muscle spasms overnight.

When his wife called the surgery the next morning the same two nurses appeared and, instead of lowering the dosage in the syringe driver, they added 15mg of Midazolam (a benzodiazepine used routinely pre-op to 'relax' the patient for surgery but it is also used in status epilepticus to paralyse the muscles to stop spasm, which is why it was used in this case; it is neither a painkiller nor a sedative).

Don's wife was told by the community nurse that he had about twenty-four hours left, so if anyone wanted to see him they should come that day, so be prepared! She was also told by the local Hospice Charity nurse specialist that she must not interact with her husband, nor hold his hand or stroke or comfort him in any way, and when she asked, "Why ever not? I have been comforting him all through his illness," she was told that if she did he would try to respond and if he came out of sedation he would be very anxious and distressed!

By this time Don was already suffering withdrawal symptoms from lack of his medications, starvation, dehydration and terror from hallucinations. The addition of Midazolam paralysing his muscles, including the diaphragm (the largest muscle in the body), and filling his lungs with fluid creates the sensation of drowning and suffocation in a patient and is equivalent to the Chinese torture of 'waterboarding' on an individual, so when Don could not cough up the congestion building in his throat due to Midazolam, these torturers then gave him hyoscine bromide to dry up the secretions, but of course it dried every other organ in the body as it went through the bloodstream like fire in the blood vessels, prompting Don's last words to his wife: "I'm on fire inside, darling, on fire inside."

This tortuous death regime lasted for six days in total, with ever-increasing bolus doses of diamorphine, Midazolam and hyoscine bromide until there was no fight left in this courageous man and finally he found peace in death with his wife by his side as she had been all along throughout this traumatic journey, unable to comfort him but hoping that he would sense that she was there with him and gain some sort of peace in his last hours of need.

It was only when Don's wife decided to question her husband's treatment it was established that the death regime had been based on the out-of-date TEP form that had been filled in by the GP and consultant two years previously in 2014 and was completely out of date, as were the JIC bag medications left on the premises and therefore not applicable as there had been no review since that date, and Don did not have pneumonia when he died but exacerbation of COPD being treated with the medications that were stopped and then the administration of noxious substances in a syringe driver!

I suggest that members of the public are very careful about filling in TEP forms either themselves or by a medical professional on their behalf and be aware that they too may be starved, dehydrated, with all means of survival taken away from them, and left to die in torment.

All the facts in this statement are true and documented and so can be verified. I would also like to add that the drugs administered to Don are the same drugs used in the USA to execute the prisoners on Death Row, and the Governor of Ohio Mike DeWine has halted all executions in the State until a new protocol is found that does not cause 'cruel and unnecessary suffering' to the inmates for execution. The longest execution was Clayton Lockett, who took forty-five minutes to die and woke up halfway through the procedure!

It took Don six DAYS to die with ever-increasing doses of the same drugs and it was called:

PALLIATIVE CARE!

ANECDOTES

Anecdotes

My Brother-in-Law

Don was a gentle character who was at best one of 'Nature's casualties'; he had done his time in National Service in the Army, and although very talented in the world of construction, he was content to spend his days doing repairs and odd jobs for the local population in and around his home area.

He lurched between times of feast and famine, refusing any help or assistance of any kind when times were hard. He was happiest at home with his wife Nellie and family of daughter and son in their little cottage up the hill from the village.

On this particular day he was cycling home from work and approaching the bridge over the river at the bottom of a steep hill. There was a pub situated alongside the riverbank in the valley where he had often called in on his way home from work. As he reached the middle of the narrow bridge, suddenly from below a mallard duck took off from the water and flew up in his face, knocking him off his bike and giving him a black eye and a cut lip in the process!

I don't know who was more surprised by the encounter. As Don got to his feet and walked over to his bike he noticed that the duck had broken its neck in the collision, so he picked it up and at that moment a couple from the pub appeared with a tot or two of brandy to steady his nerves and check his wounds.

He assured them that he was okay to get home, as the bike appeared to be in one piece, and thanked them for their assistance.

Don's wife Nellie was wondering where he was but not unduly worried as he was often a bit late on occasion. When he finally appeared in the doorway, battered and bruised, she asked, "What happened to you? Have you been drinking?"

"No, I was attacked by a duck on the way home."

When she stopped laughing she said to him, "And what state is the duck in?"

Don produced the duck from behind his back and held it aloft without a feather on it. "Oven-ready," was his reply. "We are having the b****r for dinner tomorrow!"

Anecdotes

Christmas Present

It was Christmas and everyone had gathered at Don and Nellie's for Christmas Day festivities. We settled down after lunch to open our presents, and we always gave Don little tins of snuff, a habit he had had since he was a young man, and the children were fascinated as they watched him put a pinch on the back of his hand and sniff up the powder in each nostril, and after a few minutes he would give a sneeze or two and then his breathing became easier.

This particular year we decided to play a trick on him by replacing the snuff in one of the tins with cayenne pepper! So we emptied out one of the tins and replaced it with the pepper, then resealed the lid and put it on top off the others so it would be opened first, then we all sat round waiting to see what would happen.

It seemed ages until Don finally opened up his presents and at once opened up the 'suspect' tin of snuff; he remarked that this tin's contents were a bit different in colour, lighter and finer texture than usual. "Oh yes," we said, "the man only had three tins so we got this one for you to make up the four, and the man said it was very good for sinus problems, but use a little first time until you get used to it!"

Don took a good pinch of the contents and proceeded to sniff up the 'special' snuff. A couple of very deep sniffs and all eyes were on him awaiting the result, but surprisingly nothing happened at all for five minutes and we were rather disappointed after all our efforts. However, then the eruption started…

Sneeze after sneeze resounded around the room and the spray that followed each one drove us all to seek shelter behind the sofa and chairs!

I think those tubes got rid of years of clogged nasal passages! After about fifteen minutes of mayhem the sneezing ceased and sanity prevailed once more. Ironically, as Don said later, even his taste and hearing had much improved along with his nostrils, so he forgave us for playing such a trick on him; but he was very careful when he got any presents from us in future!

Anecdotes

Dentures

Don was attending the wedding of one of his nieces and had fished out his best suit and tie for the occasion, and after much cajoling by Nellie he sported a brand-new set of dentures to complete the makeover. We had never seen him looking so smart when he turned up at the little church in readiness for the ceremony.

It was a typical village church nestling along the east side of the village, with the church hall on one side and the local pub a few yards further up on the other side. The little churchyard lay sheltered by a line of yew trees to the rear where the gentlefolk from many generations rested peacefully, separated by the grassy pathways that ran east to west the length and breadth of the site, ensuring that the morning sunrise and the evening sunset bathed the inhabitants in a golden glow.

Don decided to take a stroll along the grass pathway to look at the graves while he waited for the congregation to fill the church. As he strolled up the pathway, his hay fever got the better of him and he was overcome by a bout of sneezing. Unfortunately, the force of the last sneeze ejected his new dentures from his mouth and they sailed up into the air before falling on the grass nearby. As he bent down to retrieve his 'pearly whites', St Peter (the vicar's Jack Russell terrier) leapt forward and grabbed the dentures before making off with them up the pathway right to the other end, with Nellie in hot pursuit, saying, "Come back here, you varmint, they cost me a fortune, I'll give you St Peter!" It was at this point St Peter came to a dead end. He turned around and looked at his pursuers and gave Don a dazzling smile as he realised that the game was over. Don's response was as follows: "He can keep the b*****s, they look better on him than they do me."

At that remark, the novelty of the whole chase wore off and St Peter dropped the teeth on the grave of the old village tramp, cocked his leg on it and went home well satisfied with the day's shenanigans so far.

Safe to say, the rest of the day's festivities went without a hitch apart from the fact that Don's diet was somewhat curtailed, but he thoroughly enjoyed the soup course, having extra portions.

Anecdotes

Bicycle

Don was a familiar figure in the village as he cycled to and from work in his 'uniform' of woolly hat, long coat and boots regardless of the weather, waving to everybody he met along the way. He was not one for hobbies, being quite content to potter around his garden and get in Nellie's way indoors. His only weakness was a trip to the 'bookies' in the nearest town just three miles away to put a bet on the horses, which he enjoyed on a regular basis.

This particular day he had gone to the 'bookies' as usual, leaving his bicycle outside leaning against the lamp post as always, while he chatted away to the other eager punters within. He managed to win a few shillings which repaid his stake and a little to spare so he said a cheery, "See you next time," as he left to go home.

When he got outside he found his bicycle had gone! He looked up and down the street but there was no sign of it at all. Now in those days petty crime was unheard of in that area and people never locked their front doors or cars as everyone knew everyone else, so if they were doing anything unlawful they were swiftly apprehended by the local 'bobby' on the beat, who knew them all anyway and where they lived; so it was very rare to find criminal action going on anywhere!

Don ran back into the 'bookies' with his tale of woe, but nobody had seen or heard anything, so he was advised to go straight to the police station to report the crime, as whoever took the bike could not be that far away as it didn't go very fast to start with!

The sergeant at the station was very helpful. "What time did you leave it? Where did you go? Did you see anybody lurking about outside?" He took down all the details, sharpening his pencil two or three times in a slow, deliberate way, which irritated Don, who by now was getting worried as he was expected home and there was no telephone so he could not let Nellie know what had happened.

The sergeant said, "Just one more question about the bicycle, did it have any distinguishing marks on it at all or anything specific to help identify it?"

"No, not really, it's just a plain old black bike with no brakes and only one pedal."

"Well, in that case I would assume that we are looking for a one-legged thief, that should narrow it down a bit," was the reply, and the sergeant sharpened his pencil once more. "We'll let you know of any news as it comes in, now best get off home."

So Don started to walk home but then, luckily, one of the local farmers was driving his truck that way and offered him a lift if he didn't mind travelling in the back with the pigs he had just bought at the market. So Don clambered in and sat on a bale of straw while the pigs came to inspect this strange object in their midst; perhaps his woolly hat was tasty, so one grabbed it but found it was rather unpalatable so spat it back at him and lost interest. So he arrived home in one piece.

Having told Nellie all about his latest escapade, she was as practical as ever about it, saying that with a bit of luck whoever took the bike would come to grief as soon as he went down a steep hill and realised that the brakes didn't work, and unlike Don he would not have boots with studs in to slow the pace with one foot on the road, so not to worry too much as everyone was keeping an eye out for it and it would turn up soon.

So sure enough a few days later good news arrived about the treasured bike. It transpired that the culprits were in fact the local dustmen who were clearing the rubbish in that area on that day and had spotted the bike propped up by the lamp post because it was nearby to the bins they were emptying. After inspecting it they decided it had been left there for them to take to the tip in Newport, twelve miles away, but if he wanted to go and get it he would need wellington boots and stout gloves and he was welcome to it! And there was also a note from the police sergeant which said, "I am pleased to hear that your bicycle has been found and will be back in your possession soon, but I must warn you that if you do not repair it to a roadworthy condition I shall charge you accordingly."

We don't quite know what happened to that old bike because when Don died at home it was propped up at the bottom of his bed and when the undertakers came to remove him to the funeral parlour one said to the other, "Looks like this one's got his own transport so he won't need us!"

Anecdotes

Camping
(i)

The warm days of summer had arrived and we decided to take ourselves off and spend a few days going back to Nature away from the bustle of seaside life. You had a map, compass and a good knowledge of the stars at night, having been a navigator in military service, so we felt well equipped to cope with every eventuality!

The first task was to find a quiet lake or river to park alongside for a peaceful night under the stars, so we drove along following the map until we found the perfect spot, a large lake surrounded by shrubs and trees, so we settled down for a cuppa before we started fishing. My Toyota estate car was turned into a 'mini caravan' with foam mattress, two pillows, two sleeping bags, Bluet stove with six cylinders, one saucepan, one kettle, one frying pan and one box of groceries, and a large 'camo' sheet which doubled up as ground sheet or 'Bivi' sheet to act as a tent when required!

So after a quick meal we tackled up our fishing rods

and settled down to a quiet night by this lovely lake with tawny owls and night jars hooting and whirring overhead for company and a soft ripple on the surface of the lake as the fish swam lazily around beneath us occasionally one would take the bait and when caught it was swiftly released and returned to the depths once more, and so the evening wore on and as I looked at the shrubs in the half-light it seemed as if they were moving in unison with the breeze and I asked you if you could see the movement as well.

"Don't be silly," was your reply, "you have obviously been looking at the water for too long and your eyes are playing tricks on you!"

No sooner had you finished speaking than one of the shrubs stood upright and let forth a blood-curdling cry! And at the same time the other shrubs all rose up and charged across the lake towards us! How on earth were we to know that the local marine camp was on manoeuvres that night, so no wonder it was quiet! As the last one passed us he shouted out, "Bet you didn't expect to catch us lot, tight lines!" We were rather shaken by the experience and decided that the fish were probably a mile away by now, so we decided to call it a night and try somewhere else tomorrow.

Camping
(ii)

The following morning we decided to make our way towards Hampshire, as you had an old friend from your Oxford days who lived at Fordingbridge and rented out a strip of the River Avon to the local fishing fraternity. They were a traditional bunch who paid well for the privilege to fish there without disruption.

We arrived at Guy's Homestead, a farm in the New Forest, and were given permission to camp alongside the river away from the fly-fishing area with strict instructions not to fish nearby any paying guest and only you to fish for a brace of trout for our own use as non-members were not allowed in the area.

So you tackled up and positioned yourself on a stretch of water, and I went downstream to a small bend in the river amongst a bed of reeds and sat down out of view with my little telescopic rod and attached a fly I caught on a nearby bush to the hook and let it drift on the surface by my feet, giving it an occasional twitch, and settled down in the sunshine at peace with the world around me. Time passed and I heard voices in the distance, so I quickly hauled in my rod, folded it up and put it in the carrier bag by my side, and sat on it. I picked up my binoculars and as I did so I saw this hat appear through the reeds coming in my direction; he was obviously a fisherman because his hat had dry flies attached all round it and a fishing waistcoat with all the equipment of a 'professional piscatorial expert'.

"Good morning," he said. "I understand from your gentleman upriver that you have spotted a bar-tailed godwit down here. I haven't seen one of those around here for years this early in the season."

I immediately thought, what the hell is a bar-tailed godwit? I bet that halfwit upriver made that one up! So I blurted out, "Well, I'm not sure because I did wonder if it was too early in the season for them?"

"Yes, yes, quite, they don't usually fly up this far at this time of year."

As soon as he said 'fly' I thought, that's it, it's a bird, so I'm okay now!

"I understand that you are an ornithologist," he continued. "Where did you spot it? Which way did it go?"

"Well, I'm pretty sure it was a cock bird judging by the plumage as it flew over; unfortunately, it took off just as you approached and went in the direction of that belt of trees as there is an inlet under there and he seemed to be making for that, but you may well spot him if you take a look over there."

"Yes, I know that spot well. I'll take a look, thank you very much."

"You are very welcome, and may I ask what you do for a living, sir?"

"I am one of Her Majesty's Judges and I preside at the Old Bailey in London."

Christ, I thought, I hope you don't look in my carrier bag or I might find myself up before you on the bench for trying to poach Her Majesty's trout!

"Well, cheerio for now," he said. "Enjoy the rest of your day."

"I will indeed, goodbye."

As soon as he had left I packed up my gear and came to find you to ask why you didn't stop him from coming down to where I was! Your reply was that he had spotted me and said, "My God, there's a woman on the water!", so you told him that I was your lady and I was an ornithologist and had seen a bar-tailed godwit in that vicinity. You had no idea that he was a bird watcher himself! In any case you knew that I could talk myself out of any situation so you were quite confident about it!

"Well, have you caught any fish yet?"

"No luck at all," you replied. "They are just not biting today."

"Oh dear, well, good job I had better luck then."

"Why have you caught one?"

"No, I've caught two nice rainbow trout."

"Really? Well, where are they? They are not in your bag."

"I've got one down each wellie! Now best get out of here before the judge comes back and we will find somewhere to cook them."

Camping
(iii)

Our next camping assignment consisted of a tour of the 'Oast Houses' in the Kent area so we set off to explore the countryside in the 'Garden of England', spending our nights in bluebell-covered woodlands and waking to a dawn chorus that filled the air around us while we breakfasted courtesy of our little Bluet stove with the rustle of tiny feet in the undergrowth around us as the pale light of a new day engulfed us in its golden glow and Nature's day shift emerged to begin their hunt for survival.

We continued our tour of the countryside, taking in Canterbury Cathedral on our way around the Hop garden areas. We decided to stop overnight not far from the large 'Pinetum' owned by the Forestry Commission at Goudhurst, and as darkness fell we found ourselves in a large beech-covered woodland which was a perfect place to spend the night as it was far enough away from the Pinetum but was obviously a woodland for the public.

So we parked under a grand old beech tree and were having a 'cuppa' before settling down for the night. Suddenly, a vehicle appeared as we were relaxing; a man emerged and opened the rear door of the car and out jumped a Labrador dog. The man looked over at us and then proceeded to take the dog for a walk along the footpath and into the woodland. When he returned some time later and put the dog back in the car, he again looked across and then approached us. We thought he may be a ranger or perhaps a farmer checking his boundaries on a night patrol.

"Good evening," he said.

"Oh, good evening to you, what a lovely spot you have here," we replied.

"Are you passing through or are you staying the night?"

"Well, we were hoping to stay here as there are no notices to say no overnight parking or camping and it is such a lovely spot and we haven't seen any locals at all so it's not too busy."

"No, the locals don't come here," was the reply. "Not since the murders!"

"What!" We looked at him in amazement.

"Whereabouts?" I asked.

"Just where your car is under that beech tree, yep, last one was eighteen months ago and they haven't caught him yet. Well, good luck in case I don't see you again!" and, raising his hand in salute, he returned to his car and drove off!

We looked at one another. "Well, what do you want to do?" you asked. "Do you want to move on or take a chance with the murderer? Mind you, I don't fancy his chances if you've got that frying pan in your hand – you'll knock him out at twenty-five yards!"

"Thanks a bunch, but I'm too tired to drive any further tonight. I would be a danger to the Great British public, so we will just have to take our chances with the murderer if he turns up! Perhaps that fellow was just winding us up."

And so you decided to make plans just in case we were attacked by any roving murderers in the vicinity of our campsite! We collected thin sticks which you stuck in the ground all around the car in a circle and attached 'para cord' to each one about eighteen inches off the ground to allow foxes, badgers, etc., to go underneath, but any human being would trip over and pull on the cord which you had threaded through the back of the car and inside your sleeping bag and tied around your big toe saying that any movement would twitch your toe and wake you up!

"And then what?" I asked.

"Well, then I will wake you and you can attract his attention and keep him talking while I creep up behind him and knock him out with a blow from my folding shovel while you phone the police!"

I wasn't sure that this would work, but you said that your experience of jungle warfare in Vietnam would stand us in good stead in the English countryside and you were confident that it would all turn out fine.

And so we clambered into our sleeping bags and settled down for the night with your big toe just emerging from your sleeping bag with para cord attached to it! My sleep was fitful to say the least as I kept looking out the window at the shadows created by the moon through the trees and imagined that I could see a person standing there by the pathway while you slept soundly all night! It wasn't until dawn broke that I could make a cup of tea and get breakfast underway.

I called you and was startled by a cry of pain as you

emerged from the car and called for assistance. "Whatever is the matter with you?" I asked.

"It's my big toe, look at it…"

I looked, and sure enough, the big toe had been replaced by what looked like a large, purple Victoria plum; in short, the cord was tied so tightly around it that the circulation to the toe itself was stopped and caused the swelling and pain!

"Well, all I can say is thank God the murderer never turned up as he would have got two for the price of one as you would have been useless! So I must now cut that cord off your toe and you must soak it to get the swelling down. I'll get the scalpel out of the first aid box and cut through very carefully and you will need to rest it today and hopefully with a massage later it will be okay to move on."

And so eventually we managed to move on again and sometime later we came across a cafe where we could have a meal and stock up on food for the journey ahead. Whilst we were there we got talking to a couple at the next table and explained why you were hobbling about with a sore toe and I mentioned the fact that I thought the man in the woods was winding us up with his story of murders, but then the couple said, "Oh no, he wasn't; he is quite right – there were indeed two murders in that woodland and nobody was arrested or charged for the crimes."

So my advice to anybody who decides to camp in a woodland is this – check the details of the places you stay, and steer clear of an idiot with para cord!

Camping
(iv)

After our eventful tour of the beautiful Kentish countryside we began our return journey along the south coast of our green and pleasant land, heading in a westerly direction towards Dorset, where we visited Monkey World and met little chimp Trudy clutching her bundle of straw crouched in a corner. She had been rescued from the famous Chipperfield Circus, where she had been cruelly abused by Mary Chipperfield, who was in charge of the chimps at the time and who was successfully prosecuted at a later date for the treatment of the chimps in her 'care'. This sad-eyed little chimp gradually became a much-loved member of the troop, comforted by the other females, but the scars of her previous life affected her both mentally and physically, as were some of the other members of the group from similar backgrounds, but they found solace in each other and we could learn a lot about humanity from the animal kingdom! As the daylight faded we continued west and eventually found ourselves in a quiet country lane and upon reaching a beautiful wooded area decided that we would stay overnight and so we settled down to the hoot of a tawny owl above us and the faint scent of the distant sea and the promise of more adventures to come!

As dawn broke we emerged, refreshed and ready, for the new day. I put the kettle on and you prepared to have a shave in the wing mirror of the car. When you were about halfway through your ablutions we were suddenly interrupted by a large army staff car trundling towards us. When it stopped alongside a very smart fellow jumped out and shouted out, "What the hell are you doing?"

You were rather irritated by such a stupid question when your face was half covered in shaving cream! "Oh, good morning, as a matter of fact I'm shaving," was your curt reply!

"Do you know where you are?" he shouted.

"No, we haven't a clue."

"Didn't you see the forty-foot poles with red flags on, you idiot?"

"We are not bats, we came in at midnight, so we didn't see anything. Anyway, where are we?"

"Oh, I'll tell you where you are alright, you are in the middle of the army tank firing range at Bovingdon and my gunners open fire in ten minutes precisely, so Get Orf Now!"

You seemed unperturbed by his order and replied, "Can I finish my shave first? I am British, you know!"

"No, you bloody well can't finish your shave first – get going or I shall have you arrested, if you're still alive!"

And so we beat a hasty retreat with half your face still covered in shaving cream, and as we drove uphill overlooking Kimmerage Cove, sure enough on the dot the whole place erupted with gunfire from the approaching tanks and we could see the black and white cardboard tanks in amongst the area where we had been parked overnight! So I said, "I bet that's the closest shave you've ever had – I wonder where we shall end up next!"

Camping
(v)

And so onwards and upwards once more, we decided to go north-west to Exmoor as you wanted to reach Dunkery Beacon, the highest point in Exmoor, where the views were spectacular, taking in Dorset to the south, Devon to the west and Somerset to the east. As we reached the hilltop the clouds gathered and the views were soon obscured by the following deluge; however, we made a brew and waited until the rain finally eased off and we could take a stroll amongst the heather-clad downs. The afternoon wore on and gradually the other visitors began to disappear homeward and we were left to enjoy the last views before the daylight faded.

As we sat quietly an Exmoor ranger pulled up in his Jeep and said, "I have come to warn you that you must leave now as we do not allow anyone to stay overnight on Dunkery Beacon."

"Can we ask why you don't allow overnight parking?"

"Well," he said, "did you not see the firebreaks with wooden beaters in special containers all along the pathway? We don't want you setting the heather on fire!"

You replied, "My dear fellow, it has been pissing down solidly with rain for the last forty-eight hours. I will give you a ten-pound note if you can even get a fire started in these conditions!"

"That's not the point; it's not allowed, so I will escort you off the Beacon."

So we followed him down to the main roadway and he watched until we were out of sight.

We waited about half an hour and then decided to return to the Beacon to see the view at night, which was stunning in the clear moonlit vision after the rain, so you decided to erect the 'Bivi' tent over a bed of heather and we settled down in our sleeping bags to the scents of the fresh rain-washed countryside around us in complete peace with Nature.

Next morning I awoke to a cacophony of birdsong at dawn, and as daylight enveloped our little nest in the heather I noticed that you were not next to me, so I guessed that you were on an early patrol of the area and so I decided to make a cuppa and get ready for the day's adventures! You had still not returned so I decided to go and look for you along the paths around the area, occasionally calling out to you, but no reply. I was starting to get worried in case you had wandered off and had an accident somewhere (not unusual), so I did a circular search, making my way back to the 'Bivi'.

Suddenly, I heard a faint cry and called out, "Where are you?"

"Down here, I'm down here!"

I followed the sound and came to the edge of a steep gully filled with brambles and scrub. "What the hell are you doing down there?"

Apparently, you had rolled over in your sleep and did not realise that you were on the edge of a precipice and had rolled down, trapped in your sleeping bag, to halfway down a thirty-foot drop and ended up entrapped in the brambles, unable to move. You accused me of pushing you out on purpose when you were asleep!

"Don't be ridiculous, you should have checked the area properly first for unseen hazards before you put the Bivi up to make sure it was safe, you idiot!"

"I can't move, get me out of here!"

"Alright, I'll get the car and the towing rope and pull you up that way; at least you are protected from the brambles by the sleeping bag over your head and arms."

So I backed the car as near as possible to the edge and tied the rope to the tow bar, then abseiled down the rope and tied the other end tight around your waist, and then climbed back up again and started the engine and very slowly inched forwards to bring you up as carefully as I could amidst a torrent of very ungentlemanly comments from down below!

All of a sudden you rose like a phoenix from the ashes in an upright position looking remarkably like an Egyptian mummy from the Valley of the Kings!

"Serves you right for breaking the rules and coming back up here when we shouldn't have done – do you want a cup of tea?"

"Well, I'm feeling rather weak, but I think I can manage a cuppa if you get me out of this bloody sleeping bag. I've got cramp from being down there for so long."

"Never mind, looks like it's going to be a nice day."

"Well, it couldn't get any bloody worse, could it?" was your reply!

Camping
(vi)

We decided to shake the dust of Exmoor off our feet and travel west as far as Falmouth in Cornwall, putting the adventures of the eastern and central southern counties behind us! You decided that Cornwall was going to be far less hazardous to our health and welfare! What could possibly go wrong in the little coves and cobbled streets of our most westerly county?

So we made our way south-west, stopping off at night in lovely places along the way like Allaleigh, where you enjoyed an early morning dip in the river, where the clear water sparkled in the first rays of sunshine as it trickled its merry way to the sea.

I was already up and dressed and preparing breakfast when I heard voices coming from the direction of the river. On closer inspection I saw you in deep conversation with a lady carrying a basket of mushrooms. She seemed very intent on your naked form standing in the water and even offered you the facilities of her shower as she lived nearby! You declined her kind offer through chattering teeth, but she seemed quite happy to stand there and point out her favourite fungi from the surrounding area and offered to take you on a foraging, trip at which point you said, "Madam, before I decide to go anywhere my greatest need is to put my trousers on!"

"Oh yes, of course. Well, don't let me stop you, you just carry on!"

So you tried to cover your modesty with one hand while tip-toeing out of the rock-strewn riverbed, bending and twisting in all directions as you avoided the submerged hazards and giving the impression of a break dancer revealing all from every angle!

When you finally reached me you said, "Why didn't you come and rescue me?" so I replied, "Well, you seemed to have everything in hand when I looked!" So finally we managed to complete breakfast and, waving goodbye to your fungi-loving fan, we continued on our merry way westward.

Having finally reached the busy harbour at Falmouth, we watched the fishermen unloading their catch and the local hoteliers, restaurant owners and other traders gathered around to assess the most suitable seafood for their own use. Of course, we could not leave without sampling the local fish and chips for supper that night, and so we found a charming little place just to the north of the harbour and enjoyed a supper fit for a king and lively conversation with the owners, who had connections with the Isle of Wight (my place of birth), so we shared past memories of days gone by in another area known for its fishing fraternity, and we stayed late into the evening, and when we bade them a final farewell I asked if they could tell us of a spot nearby where we could park overnight without disturbing anyone.

"Oh yes, of course," was the reply. "Just take the uphill road towards Babbacombe and you will find some nice quiet pull-ins along the way, especially along the plateau with lovely views of the surrounding countryside."

And so we made our way following the instructions, although it was dark we felt we were on the right track, and sure enough, we found an open gateway with level grassy area, ideal for parking the car.

As we clambered into our sleeping bags you said, "Well, that was a lovely meal, and good portions too – how much did it cost by the way?"

"What do you mean? I thought you paid for it; I didn't."

"Well, no, I didn't pay; I thought you did!"

"Oh my God, we must go back tomorrow and settle up before we move on. We had such a good time; I bet they think we did it on purpose and are just fraudsters!"

Morning dawned and I wiped the steam off the windows and looked around; strewn all over the place were paint tins, an old pram and rubbish everywhere. It dawned on me that of all the places we could pick in this lovely area, we had reversed into the local landfill site and perched on the edge of the filling shute that the lorries used to empty their cargo into the pit.

I gave you a nudge to wake you up. "Look where we are," I said.

"Good God, I can see what they've been living on for weeks. Well, that's it, I can't shave here, I am British, you know, I do have my standards to keep up. We will go down to the harbour and I will shave in the gents' toilets and then we will settle up our bill at the Herring Bone."

And so back we went and parked up alongside the toilets; I watched you disappear inside and, after using the ladies' facilities, I settled back in the car to await your transformation.

As I sat there I watched a 'county-type' gent in the usual tweeds and hunting jacket enter the gents, and after a short time he reappeared in a rather agitated and flustered state; he looked across at me and then ran up the road!

Eventually you came out again and strolled towards the car with a sly smile on your face.

"What have you been up to in there? Did you scare that 'county' fellow? He came out of there like a bat out of hell. What did you say to him?"

"Well, it was like this… as you know, I came here for a shave, but there was no mirror so I was polishing the tiles with my sleeve to get a reflection when this fellow came in and asked me what I was doing – well, I thought it was obvious, so I said, 'I'm polishing the tiles.'

"'Why, are you employed by the council?'

"'No, are you?'

"'Certainly not,' he replied. 'So why are you polishing the tiles?'

"'Now, look, my dear chap, people have hobbies, don't they?' He nodded. 'Some people play golf, some like fishing or shooting.'

"'Yes, I like shooting and playing golf.'

"'Well, there you are then, so you see my hobby is polishing tiles in public toilets!'

"'But why?'

"At that point I took my cutthroat razor out of my pocket and held it up for him to see, at which point he turned very white and said I was mad and rushed off out again, so at least I had my shave in peace in the end!"

Well, after that performance we finally made it back to the Herring Bone, where we apologised for our mistake the previous evening and departed with our reputation intact and some lovely crab sandwiches to take with us on our journey, as the owner said that we had restored his faith in human nature as they had not expected to see us again! So we decided to wend our weary way back to the Isle of Wight to take some time out before our next foray into foreign parts.

LETTERS

Letters

Hi Cousins, Thank You So Much…

14th October 2018

Hi Cousins,

Thank you so much for your lovely calendar and letter. Well done, Fran, your writing is much clearer than mine, that is why I type or email, and that's as little as possible, as you will have realised by my distinct lack of communication with everybody! I know I am just an old 'has-been' these days, but what I have been is quite interesting and that's all that matters in the end!

It seems these days my presence is now required more at funerals than anything else, but I must say that the last two were quite entertaining…

My friend and neighbour lost her husband on 21st June this year and she invited me to accompany her family to the funeral and her son-in-law gave me a lift in his car. At the time my left hand and arm were in plaster and a sling, and as I got in the car I scraped my right elbow which had been grazed when I fell over, so it started to bleed profusely all over the back seat, needing an array of tissues to stop it, at which point she said, "Trust you to steal his thunder at his funeral, it's supposed to be 'his day'." Anyway, we followed the hearse to the crematorium and I was resting my left hand on the window ledge of the car; of course, I didn't realise that from the outside it looked as if I was giving an obscene V sign to all and sundry as I passed, as I had previously asked the surgeon to please leave my two first fingers free after the operation, and when he asked me why I told him, "I can't get me earrings in otherwise!"

They tried hard but they couldn't quite finish me off in hospital! Anyway, after the funeral we all went back to a local hotel for drinks and nibbles and then the son-in-law drove me back home before I bled anymore over anything else!

But the last funeral was the one to top 'em all!

Another neighbour used to visit us quite often, as she had the same illness as my husband; she died in July this year, but this time it was a church burial alongside her son who had died young many years ago.

The church was up a steep hill, and I arrived early as I didn't know what the parking would be like, so I was first into church just looking around when a lady with memorial cards approached and asked me if I knew anything about the deceased's background as they needed notes for the vicar! I suggested that she ask the funeral director as they were handling the arrangements and the information should have been passed on already.

Then the church door opened and a fellow called out, "Where's the disabled entrance?" He was directed to the west door and then they appeared, the lame, the halt and the blind, who shuffled, crawled and stumbled into the front pews, and one bright spark came up the aisle and parked her walking frame right in the middle and sat down in the pew in front of me; of course, the coffin and entourage appeared and had to wait while she got up and bent over in the aisle with her back to the coffin and folded up the frame and dragged it into the pew alongside her.

The vicar then started his introductions and said that we would sing 'Abide with Me', but unfortunately the organist had failed to turn up so he said that we would only sing the first and last verses and he would start us off!

I said to the chap next to me, "I hope you can sing as I am tone deaf."

His reply was, "Pardon? I didn't hear what the vicar said," so I turned to the people in the pew behind and apologised for what they were about to hear, which made them smile as well!

So off we went and did our best, and just as we finished the last note the church door opened and in crept the organist, who sidled up to the organ without a word; he sat down and pulled out all the stops ready for the off and was totally ignored by the vicar and not required after that.

The only notes the vicar had were the ones given to him by the husband, who proceeded to tell him how they'd got together when she was only fifteen years old, which the vicar decided he could not relate to the congregation as it was too unsavoury and illegal, so we carried on with a couple of tributes and then followed the procession up the hill to the graveside, where the close family, mourners and friends were given very large yellow dahlias to throw in the grave on top of the coffin, but it must have been very shallow as they came up over the top! At this point the last couple of mourners then reached the top of the hill on their walking frames to be met by the others coming back down as it was all over!

I did not go back for refreshments as I had had enough by that time; I was surprised that the vicar left early because if he had stayed he may have got two or three for the price of one looking at the congregation, so I thought to myself, there must be more to what remains of my life than this!

I go to visit my Don's grave every week in his little woodland; I take my flask and sandwiches in a backpack and sit on his log alongside his little tree and watch the grasshoppers and butterflies as they hop and flit amongst his Michaelmas daises now in bloom, and the birdsong overhead in the trees brings me peace while I tell about my week and how much I still miss him, but I know he will be at home in spirit when I get back, and when I go out shopping I tell him if anyone calls while I am out just haunt them until I get back!

I trust that life is treating you kindly and all doing well; I will try to keep in touch more regularly and I am pleased to report that the cats that caused my accident have not been seen in the vicinity since so it should be relatively quiet from now on.

Much love to all, etc.

Letters

Hi Everybody, I Am Still on Shank's Pony...

Hi Everybody,

I am still on 'Shanky's pony' from having my car written off in February so I have been unable to visit Don's grave for weeks as there are no buses from here to Cheriton Bishop and it would take me best part of a day to get there and back again via Exeter, and my gardening tools and muddy boots would not be welcome on public transport! So I have to wait for new 'wheels' to get me there or hitch a lift, which at my age is not a viable proposition! However, that's life and I am alive, have a roof over my head and my garden, so how lucky I am in the great scheme of things.

I am sitting here in Don's chair with a blackbird outside on the window sill feeding his fledgling on sultanas that I put out every day and the sparrows are dust bathing in my border out in the back garden with soil flying everywhere amid much excited twittering as they shuffle about between splashing about in the birdbath and the border; they are enchanting to watch and time passes easily when I am in their company (could be a good excuse for being lazy). I have never been a keep-fit fanatic and only run when chasing after a bus! If I had been meant to run for miles I would have been born with four legs like a racehorse or a cheetah!

I have seen more people pass by outside on the footpath/ cycle track than ever before since 'isolation', as they are making the most of the weather and forced time off, and all have the same idea to go for a walk or bike ride, and they are much more friendly than before because we are all in the same boat now; strange, isn't it, how adversity brings people together somehow?

Maureen advised me to get a shopping trolley but I prefer my backpack as I have little to buy just for myself, and walking to the shops is good enough exercise for me; mind you, the first time I tried it I started off a fit woman but came back looking like a question mark as I had too much weight in my pack and at that point people were panic buying so there was little left for the rest of us.

Two trolley-loads of toilet rolls were taken by one shopper and when I got back home a neighbour asked me if I had any toilet paper to spare as there was none left at the shop. I told her, "Yes, plenty, do you prefer The Guardian, Daily Express, Mirror or The Sun? Not The Times, however, 'cos the print comes off!" And when asked if I was visiting the 'food bank' if I ran out I said, not necessary, as I would be foraging in the surrounding forestry for fungi and hedgerows and streams for anything else (it's a long time since I had eel for breakfast with wild ransoms) I have two excellent books, Food for Free by Richard Mabey and Wild Food by Roger Phillips, so I'm all ready to put it into practice if and when required.

The first time I ventured out under lockdown to go to the local Co-op I covered my face with a scarf as I did not have a mask to wear at the time and was dressed in black from head to toe, and was promptly accused of trying to hold up the Post Office when I only went in for a postage stamp, so I thought that this is not a good start, but I was let off with a warning not to look so sinister in future as I made the customers feel nervous, so I ditched the scarf and donned a brighter top!

A few days later I tried my luck at the Tesco store, joining the queue which covered half the car park with strategic areas containing wipes and sanitiser sprays to clean trolley handles before entering the store, and we were monitored by the staff to ensure spacing was accurate. As I did not need a trolley I asked if it was okay to use the sanitiser spray on my hands to avoid contamination with a basket and was told go ahead, so I picked up the spray and pressed the nozzle hard; unfortunately, the nozzle was pointing over my shoulder at the time and I nearly blinded the poor woman behind me in the queue! Luckily she was the right distance behind me and her head was covered by a hood from her coat and she took it in good part when I told her that no virus would dare to attack her now and apologised profusely, I was told to move on and get out of the store without further disruption so I slunk off home as soon as possible.

And so day follows day and they all merge into one; hopefully I will soon get my new wheels and visit Don's grave again as no doubt I will need a safari suit and compass to find him as he will be well overgrown by now, but I will soon tidy him up again. Passers-by often comment on my front garden and it's nice to hear that it brings pleasure to others as they go on their way, but I just do it for my own pleasure and not for prizes or awards, just peaceful contentment.

Well, my dears, enough of my waffle; hopefully you are coming to terms with your dreadful recent experiences of the bush fires raging all around you and your home and managing to pick up the shattered pieces of your lives again. With all the chaos here it is easy to forget the tragedies going on in the rest of this world of ours, but I know that we will always have the spirit within us to recover somehow and take comfort from the fact that somewhere someone cares for us and always will.

I wish you all the luck in the world and my thoughts are always with you even if my emails are not! Take good care of yourselves, there are not many left like us – what's that you say? Thank God for that!

As always.

Letters

*Hi Cousins, So Pleased to Hear
You Are Enjoying Life…*

Hi Cousins,

So pleased to hear you are enjoying life in your new surroundings, dears, and as it's smaller than the Broulee house that means less dusting and cleaning, so I'm all for that, and the get-togethers on Friday nights with the neighbours sound great, so I think you have finally cracked it, so enjoy your well-earned easier lifestyle, and having the family close by is another bonus. Hopefully you have left behind the traumas of recent years and gain a sense of peace of mind again; well done both of you.

In fact I myself am considering moving closer to Cheriton Bishop (where Don is buried) and leaving this little bungalow behind where we spent our last years together; it is a battle between head and heart, and my head says stay here as I have everything I need close by – for example, shops, doctor's surgery, easy access to Exeter by bus or train, and my garden that I spend most of my time in, and of course my memories of my time with Don, but then on the other hand my country roots are calling me back to the solitude and peace that I can only find away from the bustle of seaside life, to wake up to the dawn chorus again and step outside to smell the freshness in the air of a new day and look across fields again, and maybe get my second and third books underway!

Unfortunately, being a 'Gemini' I always have a dilemma about things as I see all points of view, but maybe Destiny will point me in the right direction eventually as she has done before against all advice!

I had a DNA test done for my birthday courtesy of my family; when I asked them why they chose such a gift for me their reply was, "We wanted to know who the hell you were and where the hell you came from!"

Unfortunately, when I got the results I could not read them as I had to take out and pay for a plan first before I could get into the system to view them which I have not done yet, but it threw up Steve's name as cousin, so that's where he found out that I was on the site.

I have been researching my maternal grandfather Charles Butt from the Isle of Wight as he was a property owner and keen gardener who used to show fruit and flowers at Chelsea every year, so I guess that's where I get my gardening 'gene' from, and also way back he had an Irish connection as he was ship's carpenter on the 'Guinness boats', and that's where he invested his money and became a property owner on the Isle of Wight, and even further back there was an Irish knight called Sir Butt with his own Coat of Arms, but I hope his first name was not Walter as that would make him Sir Walter Butt (hence another reference to gardening)! That will amuse S..., I'm sure; tell him I am not surprised that he has drawn a blank on the male side as we are a very vague family all round!

In fact (my first Husband), Jim Harbour was not Jim at all, but I didn't find that out until years later when I saw his birth certificate, which was something entirely different! Then after he died along came Harold Simm husband number two; we were never 'churched' as he was married to a Roman Catholic who refused to divorce him, so we had a 'slave marriage'; we jumped the broomstick and that lasted seventeen years until his death.

Then along came the last and deepest love of my life, Donald Holman but he was born Donald Thurston in London and adopted by Fred Holman, the Coalman of Exmouth, when he was eleven years old, having been evacuated to Exmouth when he was just four years old and never went back again as his mum died of TB.

So things are not always what they seem; no wonder it's so difficult to trace anybody as they are never who they should be! So good luck Steve! In fact, I'm not even sure who I am, as Maureen and I were so different in every way so I could be anybody! I remember being introduced as 'The Foster Girl' when I was a child, so I thought my name was 'Foster' – not a good start!

We have to laugh at life because we cannot change it, and when you are a no body nothing is ever expected of you, so you can be anything you want to be in your imagination, so, enter the Queen of Sheba! What a wonderful comedy it would make!

I will sign off for now, dears, so take good care of yourselves and not too much noise on Friday nights as you roll home.

Letters

Hi Cousins, My First Date for Operation…

My first date for operation was cancelled and rescheduled for 2nd August.

It was quite a big operation (won't go into details); just suffice to say that the organs in my abdomen had to be re-aligned to the proper places as they had all collapsed and were out of 'sync' due to the heavy physical work I have done all my life and think that I still can!

But I must say that my foray into surgery was interesting to say the least! I arrived on time at the hospital (7.30am) for morning 'op' and took a seat in the clinic, having had a last meal and drink at 11.30pm the previous night. I sat and waited, and eventually a nurse approached and apologised for the long wait as the surgeon was not starting 'operating' until 12.30pm and I could go home and come back again. I said, no, thank you, I will wait here as I cannot eat anything anyway! So I waited and 12.30pm came and went, as did 1.30pm; at last the doc's secretary appeared and sat down to tell me that he was not starting until 2.30pm!

I asked her if he was a good surgeon.

"Oh, yes, he is excellent," and then she added, *"He is a musician, you know, classical, plays the trumpet."*

"Really" I wondered what on earth that had to do with my operation; perhaps he was going to play 'God Save the Queen' on me tendons! Still, I thought the stiches would be neat with such flexible fingers!

Anyway, eventually at 3.30pm I was taken down to the anteroom next door to the theatre, where there were six of them all in their 'scrubs' awaiting me so I asked, "Which one is Doctor M. Taylor?"

"That's me," came the gruff reply from the fellow at the bottom of the bed.

"I understand that you are a musician?"

"Who told you that?"

"Oh, I have my sources, you know. I understand you play the trumpet?"

"I do."

"Well, may I say something?"

"What's that?"

"Well, on my way into theatre I would like 'The Arrival of the Queen of Sheba', and on my exit the 'Trumpet Voluntary' would be very nice, but if that is not possible anything suitable will do as long as it's not 'The Last Post'!"

Of course, this caused much amusement amongst the 'ranks' waiting, so he turned to the anaesthetist and said, "Just get her in there, will you?"

When I eventually woke up and felt for my scar on my tummy there wasn't one anywhere, but I knew from the pain that something had occurred! So when he duly appeared later I said to him, "What happened to the scar?"

"Oh no, it's all been done by robotics; a lot of scar damage inside there and I had difficulty in finding your pelvic ligament."

So I said, "Well, if you had told me I would have found it and polished it for you!"

"I knew I was going to have trouble with you, but now you do as you're told."

"When can I climb my palm tree? It needs tidying up."

"Not for twelve weeks," was the reply. "First of all you will need to drink seven jugs full of water straight away and when we are confident that everything is working properly you can go home after the catheter, etc., has been removed."

I was supposed to be in for three or four days, but in actual fact I was told that I could go home the next day as things had gone very well.

Unfortunately, my friend who took me into hospital was not expecting me to be released so soon and was not available to pick me up, so I asked the staff nurse to call a taxi for me, but none available, so in the end I said that I would go home on the bus; I had brought my backpack with me for my bits and bobs so thought I would be okay with that, but Sister had other ideas! "You are not going home on a bus; you do realise that you have just had a major operation, woman? I will find you some transport, you will be taken to dispatches and someone will pick you up from there and take you home."

I didn't like the sound of 'dispatches' much; I felt rather like a parcel at the Amazon depot waiting to be collected off the shelf by a delivery driver, and sure enough, there they were all sat round awaiting 'pick-up', so I was dumped amongst them awaiting my delivery!

Eventually, this very weak and weedy-looking character arrived pushing, or should I say hanging, on to a wheelchair, and I thought, My God, I hope he's not for me, but of course he was! He hardly had the strength to stand upright, so I thought, if I get on a slope I've got no chance of stopping! But he called out my name, so that was it! He struggled over and said would I like to get in the chair and he would take me out to the car but he was a bit slow! So I said, "To be honest, they did tell me to get mobile as soon as possible so I suggest that I put my backpack in the chair and you push that and I will potter alongside you." He looked very relieved and so we shuffled off in the direction of the car park. As it turned out he had come from Sidmouth as he was a voluntary reserve driver only used in emergencies; however, following my directions we duly got back about 6.30pm and he carried my backpack and we hung on to each other and arrived home like a pair of matelots returning to ship after a night ashore!

He insisted on waiting on the doorstep until I was safely ensconced inside and I watched him as he swayed his way back to his car and drove off.

It wasn't until I made a cuppa and went to take pain relief I realised that I had been sent home without any! Luckily, I have paracetamol in stock and I found some codeine tablets given to me when I had sepsis, so I took those instead and rang the surgery next day, who delivered the required meds, luckily the same ones that I had taken the night before! It's coming up on four weeks now and I am doing okay and walking to shops and back, albeit slowly, and no longer taking codeine, just paracetamol when required and doing what the old body will allow and amusing the locals with my stories!

And on that note I trust that you and family are coping with whatever life throws at you with the 'gusto' that you always have, my dears, and always will keep safe, lots of love to you all.

Xxx

Letters

The New Secretary

Director General Funeral Directors Exmouth
Devon
20th February 2000

Dear Sir,

Further to our latest communication, I trust your latest funeral service went according to plan.

Fortunately the expected rain forecast did not materialise and therefore all personnel should have remained dry. Of course, I cannot speak for the bearers, as rumour has it that one or two of them are very rarely dry, especially around The King's Head or The Pig & Whistle!

However, we must forgive the odd misdemeanour and compliment them on saving the day when the Very Reverend Father Twitchit tripped over his hassock and sprawled in front of the congregation, showering the front pew with Holy water, prompting one elderly worshipper to awake with a start and proceed to sing 'for those in peril on the sea'.

At this point the bearers concerned gently guided the

elderly gentleman to the rear of the church and seated him alongside the west door in the hope that the prevailing wind would be of benefit to his revival.

Luckily all ended well with liberal quantities of communal wine being swiftly dispatched by all parties.

I trust that this meets with your approval, if not, Get Stuffed!

Yours sincerely,
The New Secretary!

Letters

The Editor 1

It is inevitable that from the day we are born we commence to die from whatever Fate has in store for us. As far as I know there is no report that informs us of the total number of deaths per day, be it from disease, natural or other causes; we only hear of specific deaths by coronavirus infections daily.

No doubt we would be very surprised at the total number of deaths occurring around us daily due to various other reasons, for example: deprivation, starvation, cruelty, accident, cancer, heart and many other diseases.

I only watch TV news once a day in the evening because if I watched every broadcast, bulletin, report, argument or directive, I would spend what is left of my life on this planet in a permanent state of doom and gloom!

Having lost my husband to terminal illness, being unable to see my family for three years and being in lockdown on my own, I still intend to 'live' what is left of my life and not just exist in misery.

It is not the amount of time we have on this planet but the quality of the life we have, so perhaps if we are able to do so under present regulations, let's cherish what we have now and have had in the past, and one day hopefully soon this pandemic will be just a memory as well, but daily death will not cease from whatever the cause may be.

TOPICAL

Topical

Immigration
The Migrant's Story

My land is a beautiful land of ancient history, hot sunny days and cold nights, sand dunes and mountains where the wild lanner falcon hunts his prey amongst the ever-changing eternal movements of the shifting sands and where the oasis provides the miracle of water, creating a lifesaving respite amongst the endless landscape of sky and sand.

This was my home, and my forefathers before me for many generations; we lived peacefully in tune with all the wonders around us in this timeless land. We bartered our goods at the markets and bazaars along the way as we traversed this great wilderness where the myriad stars seemed low enough to touch and our forefathers were the first to map the heavens as they navigated their way across the terrain we called our home.

Then one day a change descended upon us and destroyed that serenity which we had taken for granted for so long. A new power took over our lives that came from intruders from foreign lands, and corruption and chaos took over, dominated by a government greedy and willing to sacrifice their own people for their greed and prosperity.

They came in waves of destruction by air, land and sea, bringing death, fear and carnage with them. No one was safe anymore; our homes were destroyed, our way of life taken from us, and we were scattered and divided as a people and as a nation, and so we had to flee for our lives when we were set upon by bombs from the air, tanks from the land and missiles from the sea.

We had no time to bury our dead or grieve for our loved ones; we had to hide during the day and travel by night to reach the border, where we might find sanctuary with another nation in another country.

And so began the nightmare of constantly moving on as one by one the camps that were set up for us filled up and overflowed, so there was no food or water to spare, just move on and on, scraping by on our knowledge of the land itself to keep us alive while we went from one disaster to another and another until we were far from our homeland and everything we had known and loved.

We had heard that in a far country they would take 'refugees' (as we were now called) and give us a place to live and find work for us to do, but how to get there was the problem?

After many days of wandering in hostile conditions we arrived at a large camp full of people like ourselves, just waiting for a chance to escape to a new life somewhere, anywhere, away from the carnage that had once been our home.

In one of the camps word got about that if we paid enough money, when we reached the coast we could get a boat to take us to safety to a country that would take care of us and find us work and give us houses that had fresh water for baths or showers and electricity and gas for light and cooking and our children could go to school and learn the language and have a prosperous life. It would not be like our homeland, but we would be safe to live without fear as a family again, so our goal was to reach this land of hope at all costs, this land called the United Kingdom, where everyone was welcome!

So we were approached by a man asking for money and if we had any; he could get us all passage on a boat to cross the sea or hide in the back of a vehicle carrying goods to this land of promise and safety.

My family talked about the dangers involved in this perilous journey, but we had come this far, so my two sons decided that they would try to get there in a large haulage truck which had two spaces available, and we paid the amount asked by the people traffickers, as it gave us a chance for some of us to get over to the land we desperately needed to reach.

This left my wife and two little girls to come with me on the boat and cross the strip of water known as the Channel. We had been told of many of our people, hundreds a day, reaching the United Kingdom successfully and going underground to join up with others who had gone before, and they would meet us on the other side, and the crossing was only like crossing a large lake so we were confident that we would make it safely.

We finally reached the coast under cover of darkness and found, hidden in the rocks around the headland, large inflatable rafts, and people were already scrambling to get aboard and push off out to sea without any knowledge of seamanship or tides or undercurrents or other vessels out in the shipping lanes who could not see them as they bobbed around like corks on the surface, dangerously overloaded and unstable, a disaster waiting to happen.

We were very hesitant to clamber aboard, but others were behind us and we would have missed this chance of a peaceful life, albeit in a strange land, which we could see in a faint light on the horizon, so we climbed aboard, my wife clutching our youngest child, still a babe in arms, and I took the older one and held her tight against me and I saw the terror in her little face as she clung to me and asked, "Are we going to die, Daddy?"

"I don't know, little one, but we are together, and that is all that matters, just hold on as tight as you can and may God go with us."

We drifted out into the middle of the Channel and suddenly the water around us started to churn up, a white foam from a vessel approaching our little armada of rafts and unable to see us in the darkness; it ploughed a furrow right through the middle, causing three rafts to overturn and empty their human cargo into the sea. The screams of my drowning kinsmen and women and children will haunt me all my life; there was nothing I could do to save them, and when the ship realised what had happened, it veered off away from us and disappeared into the night.

The survivors in the sea around us tried to board the other rafts but were pushed away as they were already overloaded and the extra weight would have capsized them as well.

Eventually other ships in the area came to investigate the situation. One vessel stopped and took as many people on board as it could then turned around and headed back to where the refugees had come from so they were back where they started with no money to pay for a further attempt to escape; I don't know what happened to them eventually.

We drifted on towards the faint light on the horizon and then saw a large naval vessel approaching us, churning up the seas as it slowed down to allow us to get close enough to climb up the rope ladders dangling from the sides of the ship as they beckoned us aboard.

In the following chaos our raft became awash and started to sink, so I grabbed a rope and felt myself being hauled up, and as I bumped against the ship my little one lost her grip and fell back into the sea; I wanted to jump back in to try to save her, but I was held and dragged aboard the ship. That was the last I saw of my wife and family. If we had stayed in our homeland we would have died together on our own soil, but the chance of survival drove us to try this journey; my only hope is that my sons have arrived safely at their destination and would have the chance of a new life in that land of opportunity, the United Kingdom.

As the ship took on board all she could I curled up on deck under a blanket someone had given me; I was devoid of all feeling or emotion to thank my rescuers. Why had I been saved when those I loved had not? I didn't care what happened to me now as I had no reason to live. We arrived at the port of Dover and were herded into a 'holding area', where details were taken and food was provided for us. We had to stay in these conditions until we were 'processed' and decisions made with regards our fate to be accepted in the United Kingdom or returned to where we had embarked on our fateful voyage.

Whilst we awaited our fate we watched the great container vehicles as they drove out of Dover to wherever they were destined to go, and eventually I found out that the vehicle my sons had travelled in had been found in a layby; it was noticed by the local people, who notified the authorities, and when they arrived and opened up the back of the vehicle thirty-four bodies were removed from it as it was airtight, so they all suffocated where they were left to die by the people traffickers, my sons among them.

My Destiny now lies in the hands of strangers, but I do not 'live' anymore; I just exist with my memories of that land that bore me and my family, and I shall never see either again.

Would I do the same again? I cannot answer that question as so many of my countrymen and -women are making that perilous journey right now as we speak.

There must be another way!

Topical

The Native's Story

I was born here in the United Kingdom just after the Second World War; there was still rationing of goods and butter was a luxury, so bread and margarine was the staple of our diet and chicken was a delicacy reserved for special occasions like Christmas. Life was hard for families and there were many orphans because of the war. At four years old I was put into a Roman Catholic Convent School and told that I was a sinner and destined for Hell by these black-habited shadowy figures who glided along cold marble corridors, silent except for the jangling crucifixes and rosaries hanging from their waists, and when they smiled at you it was with a cold, glassy stare without warmth or feeling of any kind.

There was a building nearby used to house single pregnant women and girls who had become pregnant through ignorance or ill use; they were treated dreadfully and when their babies were born they were taken from them and sold to mainly American childless couples who could afford the sums of money demanded by the convent for a child. They were told that the mother had died in childbirth and the mothers were told that their babies had died and were then dismissed by the nuns and sent back to where they came from.

The babies who were not claimed by prospective parents were shipped to Australia or other colonies as soon as they were old enough to populate these areas in a bid to ensure that the Great British Empire remained at the figurehead of the country involved.

I was 'fortunate' enough to be 'fostered out' to various places; in fact, I had four foster homes in a year when I was nine because the British people needed money after the war so took in 'stray children' and were paid by the Social Services of the day. So I grew up in 'care', as they called it, and survived into adulthood having grown very self-reliant and suspicious of 'Godly' people.

I married at seventeen years old and had five babies in seven years, one of whom died before he was born, but my remaining son and three daughters grew up into caring, hardworking individuals with their own families in a close-knit community.

We have a population of many different cultures and religions who make up the polyglot society that we know today.

We have donated billions of pounds over the years in foreign aid to poorer nations. Of course, when we joined the European Common Market all our produce had to go through the European Union, and our own fishing fleets were not allowed to fish in our own waters, but foreign fleets were able to use deep-sea trawlers to sweep everything from the sea bed upwards all around our shores, putting our own fleets out of business and raising the living costs of our population.

This had the effect of forcing wives and mothers into the labour market to make enough income to pay rent, mortgages and household bills, leading to a generation of 'Latchkey children' who spent most of their lives unsupervised and without respect for anyone or anything.

The immigrant population was still rising and causing unrest and friction amongst the different factions and cultures in our country, and all the time people were arriving all around our shores, putting a drain on our resources, and we continued paying donations to 'foreign aid' of billions of pounds per year.

The infrastructure of our society began to crumble under the weight of the flood of refugees, arriving from every country overrun by warlords and military coups around the world.

And then there came the pandemic! At some laboratory in another country a deadly virus was allowed to escape into the environment, the like of which had never been seen before, and spread rapidly, making it a global threat that had to be addressed by all powers to give us any hope of survival. Restrictions were put into place; vaccines were hastily produced in the hope of preventing the spread of the COVID disease. The NHS was totally unprepared for such a situation and chaos reigned for a time until tough decisions were taken to stem the flow of infection that was devastating our population. So lockdown and isolation and vaccination were introduced, Aircraft were grounded, transport stopped, everything including freight and haulage ceased, shops closed, high streets empty, schools closed and isolation was complete while the death toll continued to rise daily worldwide.

These catastrophic events changed our way of life completely; those people who could work from home did so, but those who could not lost their jobs due to isolation and without income they were unable to pay for the basic things like food, water, heating and, of course, rent or mortgage to keep a roof over their heads because many landlords/landladies relied on the rent from their property to pay their own bills as that was their only income, so they had no choice but to evict the tenants and find someone who could pay the rent.

So many families were made homeless and ended up on the streets or split up and their children taken into 'care' by the local authorities. Food banks were introduced to prevent starvation, and a feeling of fear and hopelessness engulfed the nation and left deep scars on the native population.

But still the immigrants arrive in their hundreds daily around our coasts in their makeshift rafts and boats, unhindered by the European countries that actively encourage the migrants to leave their own shores to come to this land of ours, where they slip in unseen and go underground to find their own kinfolk already here.

In the case of becoming sick with COVID variants, as

they are not vaccinated against the disease or in the system to be offered the vaccine, the total population with COVID cannot be calculated because we have no idea how many people are now carrying the virus and are not registered here. We cannot cope with our own native population, let alone a flood of incoming humanity. It is not a question of lack of sympathy but the lack of the capacity to provide for everybody who wants to come here when our own people are living on handouts from food banks and the infrastructure is crumbling around us. If we cannot progress soon we shall end up with a civil war on our hands in our own land.

Topical

The Solution

It seems to me a strange paradox when you have a situation as follows:

A country with a strong religious culture ruled by a despotic dictator as leader or a military-ruled state with an equally harsh regime (to which we have sold the arms to support their coup) now governing the population.

The people are aware of the world outside their existence and the freedoms that it offers in contrast to their present situation, so they wish to cut the ties that bind them to their existence with the help of the 'foreign liberal powers' who become involved in their internal affairs in the hope that they themselves will profit from the downfall of the leadership and gain rights to the country's valuable natural assets.

Stop selling 'arms' to foreign nations for them to use against us in future attacks!

Stop getting involved in other nation's internal affairs by assuming that our way of life is the best and only way for everyone to live regardless of culture, race or creed, the object being to profit from the country's natural assets in our race to be the first to make a deal regardless of the consequences of such actions to remain a top power on the world stage. Look where it's got us so far!

We are no longer the Great British Empire on which the sun never set as we were in Victorian times. When there was trouble the cry went up, "Send a gunboat," to quell any uprising anywhere in the empire.

Now we are just an appendage off the coast of Europe with rumblings of self-government within our own shores, and if the result of that is the breakup of Great Britain as we know it and we have our own factions, where will that lead?

I think that we will find that our charity must begin at home and then when our own population is secure we may be in a position to assist others.

Our own infrastructure needs dramatic changes to improve the lives of our own population and not allow untenable duties to every underdog that appears on the horizon to sway us as we are no longer the 'milch cow' of the world as we have been in previous times.

We have the best inventors, scientists, financial heads, artisans and workers in this country, and we need to use them to regain our own status to ensure we leave our nation with good prospects for future generations to build on and not a polyglot society that has no allegiance at all to the land that rescued them but instigates terrorist activities and the alienation of our young people for purposes of wars in their own land and ours, the land that gave them refuge here in the first place!

Topical

Pandemic

I have discontinued watching, listening to or reading about the coronavirus or COVID-19 except to hear the latest update from the local public in my area (Devon). It seems to me that since this 'pandemic' arose the world has gone mad, and the nation's attention and effort has culminated in five minutes' mayhem of standing on doorsteps, balconies and garden gates clapping hands, banging saucepan lids or anything else they can find, blowing whistles, letting off fireworks, etc., in some misguided effort of support towards the NHS. One wonders what they hope to achieve with this brief demonstration of togetherness; after all, as I understand it, when you train as a nurse, doctor or any other medical position you hold, this is what you are actually trained for and paid to do, and therefore you expect to come into contact with infectious patients and treat them as well as any other patient in your care regardless of age, status or any other circumstances. I am sure that Florence Nightingale would have preferred to just get on with the job in hand; after all, less than two years ago the NHS was crumbling before our eyes as it was impossible to get an appointment with your own designated GP within three weeks of your enquiry and much longer if you required a hospital appointment or surgical operation and we are now encouraged to purchase our own medications from the local chemist or supermarket as the NHS cannot afford to supply them to the public who have paid in advance through their taxes all their working lives to ensure they would be looked after from 'cradle to grave', as was the original intention of the NHS!

Another aspect of the 'higher echelons' of the NHS appears to be the emergence of the 'specialist nurse' taking over the role of the GP, for example now prescribing medications for various patients and taking over the completion of the updated TEP (non-resuscitation) forms and procedures for end-of-life patients and carrying them out personally! I find this change very disturbing and open to abuse of power by unqualified staff, and presumably it will lead to patients being not put on the list of a GP when they apply to a medical practice but a nurse in charge of their healthcare! The object of this will be no doubt to ease the burden of the overworked GP and lower the cost of healthcare provided to the community. If nurses are considered qualified to take over the overall care of patients, why have they not continued in their studies and passed the appropriate exams to become GPs in the first place?

I am amazed at how quickly hospitals have sprung up to accommodate the expected influx of COVID-19 patients to fill them at the expense of other patient's treatments and procedures, i.e. cancer, heart surgery, other respiratory illnesses, etc., who have all been put on hold to make way for COVID-19 victims only.

If we look back a generation, the many 'cottage hospitals' filled a much-needed role; for example, they acted as convalescent homes for patients who, although not needing specialist care from the general hospital, were not deemed well enough to return home because of passing on infection to others or they needed extra care for a while to regain their strength.

These local hospitals also served as isolation units in themselves, run by the same staff that attended the same ward and did not go off to another ward every couple of days spreading infection to vulnerable patients in other sections of the same building as now occurs on a regular basis.

Every day we see medical staff in the local shops and supermarkets wearing the uniforms they have worn whilst tending to their hospital patients instead of changing into other clothing and leaving their uniforms in the hospital environment or taking them home to launder as in previous regulations; after all, plastic aprons, gloves and masks, etc., only give certain protection and now are being discarded in their millions everywhere you go – what about reducing our waste output, not increasing it?

In fact, trying to treat all patients under one large conglomeration will never be successful, as mixing a large population of a myriad different diseases, infections, operations and procedures is for one reason only: to make the patients travel long distances to see the appropriate medical professional and to make it more difficult or at times impossible for the next of kin to visit these patients during their stay in hospital.

The death knell of the NHS as we knew it came about with the instigation of the various 'health trusts' that took over the running of the health service, and patient priority has gone downhill ever since; the days of having your own doctor available to visit and care for you and your family, knowing their patients personally for most if not all their lives, are long gone, and the only method of patient assessment is to look at a computer screen (not always updated with the patient's progress) and no personal knowledge of the patient at all.

The whole health service needs emergency surgery to stem the haemorrhage of money thrown at it, and the running of hospitals taken out of the myriad 'health trusts', and proper management, training, including 'barrier nursing', and an overhaul of general nursing, cleaning and admin staff to a standard that spans every hospital in the country, which can only be achieved by downsizing these great 'supermarket hospitals' so that individual attention can be provided by the use of regular staff on wards, and specific problems like COVID-19 are treated in hospitals designed to provide that treatment and not try to control it piecemeal in some multifunctional establishment which cannot cope with it and returns infected patients to spread throughout the community, for example, in care homes!

We now hear of discontent and possible strike action

by NHS staff due to the 1% then 3% pay rise offer by the Government; I would like to point out that thirty-three million pounds has just been donated to the NHS thanks to the staunch efforts of Captain Sir Tom Moore – where is it? I would presume that it has gone to the staff considering strike action? And what about all the other donations that are following on in the wake of Sir Tom's efforts, where are they?

And if there is a shortfall in donations from the Great British public maybe it is worth considering that many families have lost their jobs through lockdown and therefore have no income at all, and also have the threat of homelessness because they cannot pay their rent or bills, resulting in more families on the streets and children taken into 'care' because of this pandemic; I am sure they would grab 3% of anything with both hands and rejoice in the fact that they had a job at all!

And what about all the key people, the police, fire service, coastguards and, of course, our military personnel, who also put their lives on the line every day to keep us safe?

And finally, let us remember that men, women and children are dying every minute of every day from deadly infections the world over; sadly this will not stop when this pandemic is long forgotten.

Topical

Gender

When the introduction of the emancipation of the female of our species was introduced, we also succeeded in the ensuing emasculation of the male of our species, resulting in a generation of genderless people unsure of what they are supposed to be! So the line and characteristics of both sexes has been blurred and all distinguishing images have been reversed; for example, women now dress in unfeminine clothes, tracksuits and trainers, which are ideal for track events or visits to the 'gym' and hiking, etc., but where are the clothes that flatter the female form and make us proud of our femininity, as indeed we should be? And likewise, the male population is now more interested in facial, hair and skin products, and unisex and designer clothing.

No wonder there is an increase in mental health problems in the younger generation; how can they possibly function as adults when they don't even know what gender they are supposed to be, regardless of the genitalia they were born with, and the parental roles are so mixed up they don't know who is the appropriate male or female role to follow!

I agree with the principal of equality in work and pay, etc., so if a woman wishes to be a bricklayer or some other male-oriented trade or profession she is able to do so, but why must she literally become one of the 'boys' in dress, language and aggression? And equally, if a man wishes to take up a post selling lingerie or needlework, that's fine, but he does not need to lose his masculinity in doing so (sailors were excellent at sewing and knitting when away at sea but still remained 'male').

During the Second World War when the men were away fighting, the women took over the responsibility of keeping the important trades, professions and the war machine going, and did so very successfully, and so began the important input of female labour which has culminated in today's female rights of equality, but at no time did those females lose their femininity and were proud of their achievements without becoming 'pseudo males' in dress or manner, and likewise the men were not emasculated by having a capable woman for a wife or mother as the roles were still defined as male or female.

The nanny state we now live in dictates what we can or cannot say or do for fear it will cause offence somewhere along the line and crazy, mixed-up children will grow up into crazy, mixed-up adults, so I am grateful for the good memories I have of the society that I grew up in, for at least I knew the difference between the male and female roles which provided a guideline to the children of the day as to where they fitted in, whereas now we have a totally unreal existence of a genderless society of robotic individuals who do not have a clue who or what they are or how to cope with feelings they encounter throughout their existence on this planet.

I expect many more situations of mental and psychological problems in future generations as they struggle to define who or what they are supposed to be to fit in with the sexless, robotic society of today.

We do not have the freedom of speech or thought for which we fought two world wars but a continually increasing doctrine of who we should or should not be and what we are expected or encouraged to do; for instance, we have the modern religious practice of keeping 'fit' rammed down our throats by way of TV instructions from a mythical being called Peloton, who demands that we have machines in our homes that we use to run, pedal, stretch and push our bodies to the limit of physical endurance and then collapse in a post-orgasmic state on the floor to recover!

In fact, this produces the exact opposite effect of a healthy body and mind; putting all that extra strain on the body reduces the immune system's capabilities for fighting off infections and diseases and culminates in chronic problems both muscular and organic in years to come.

Ask any chiropodist who has the worst affected feet and they will say athletes and dancers, the most common complaints being with feet, ankles, knees and hips.

All this extreme activity is for one reason only and that is to take them away from the mundane, lacklustre, frenetic, discontented lives they lead and which they must return to after their 'workout' as they bask in the feel-good factor of the adrenaline rush achieved in aimless pounding on the treadmill or pedalling on a static bike in the front room or gym.

Nature gave us two good legs to walk with, and when used properly they will ensure that our bodies keep healthy, not so-called fit but in good condition for the peak performance of all aspects of physical, mental, emotional and psychological wellbeing, and for any adrenaline fix a good sex life without hang-ups and inhibitions results in the best feel-good factor of all in a healthy body, mind and spirit.

For, if you transgress the laws of Nature she will put you on your back with mathematical certainty.

So maybe, a little less of the confrontational attitude and hyper-sensitivity and more acceptance from all sides of the spectrum could result in a happier and more contented existence all round?

So, whatever category we find ourselves in, I say, "Vive la difference."